Nicky and the Twins
The Great Nappy Disaster

First published in hardback in Great Britain by HarperCollins Publishers Ltd in 1998
First published in Picture Lions in 1998

1 3 5 7 9 10 8 6 4 2
ISBN 0 00 664512-7

Picture Lions is an imprint of the Children's Division, part of HarperCollins Publishers Ltd
Text copyright © Tony Bradman 1998
Illustrations copyright © Susan Winter 1998
The author and illustrator assert the moral right to be identified
as the author and illustrator of this work.
A CIP catalogue record for this book is available from the British Library.

Printed and bound in Singapore by Imago.

Nicky and the Twins

The Great Nappy Disaster

Tony Bradman & Susan Winter

PictureLions
An Imprint of HarperCollinsPublishers

Nicky had a problem.

The Twins' birthday was coming up soon, and she wanted to give them something really special.

But she couldn't think what that special something should be. All they seemed to want at the moment was... a nappy change!

Nicky asked Dad for two nappies
to play with.

She didn't do much playing though. She sat and thought till her head ached... and still didn't get any ideas.

At bedtime, Nicky put the nappies away with her dolls.

The next day, Mum was
going to the shops to
buy the Twins'
birthday
presents.

"Why don't you come too, Nicky?" she said.

Nicky just nodded her head. She emptied her piggybank but there wasn't enough money for anything really special.

That evening, Nicky didn't do much playing.
She sat and thought and thought till her head
ached... and still didn't get any ideas.

Mum and Dad couldn't help. They were
in a tizzy; the Twins were keeping them
very busy.

The next day, Nicky went to playgroup.
"Why don't you paint
your brothers a picture?"
Mrs Robinson said.
Nicky just nodded
her head.

She sloshed on
the paint...

...but it turned out her picture wasn't anything really special.

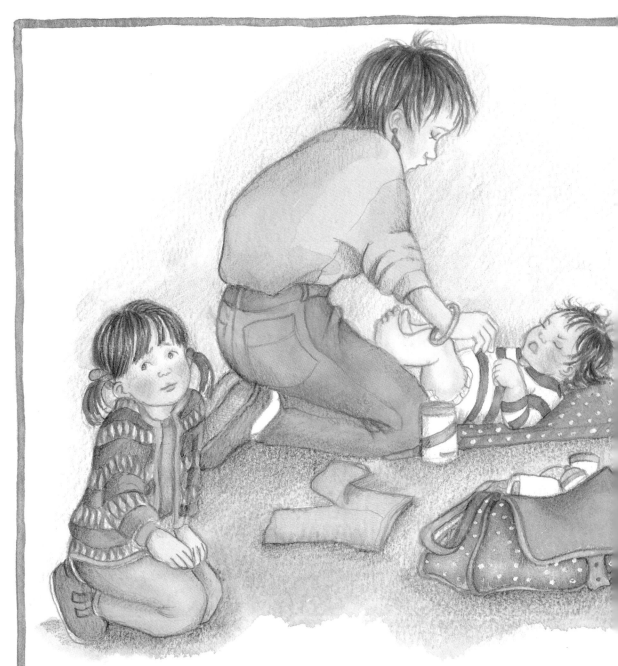

That evening, Nicky didn't do much playing.
She sat and thought and thought and
thought till her head ached... and still didn't
get any ideas.

Mum and Dad couldn't help. They were
in a state; the Twins needed clean nappies,
and they hated to wait!

The next day, Nicky's friend Anna came
to play.

"Why don't you make them a present?"
Anna said.

Nicky just nodded her head.

She rummaged and
cut and stuck...

...but what she
made definitely
wasn't anything
really special.

That evening, Nicky didn't do much playing. She didn't do much thinking, either. It was too late for that.

She sat and felt rather gloomy.

Mum and Dad couldn't help. They didn't know what to say.

And the Twins needed changing again, anyway.

The next day came, and it was the Twins'
birthday! The guests started to arrive for
the party.

And with every ding-dong on the bell, the Twins got a card – and a present as well!

Nicky just kept out of the way.

But something was wrong. The Twins were unhappy.

Then Mum and Dad realised they'd RUN OUT OF NAPPIES!

Disaster had struck – two babies were sore!

Now who is that
slipping out
of the door?

Nicky dashed
upstairs and into her
room. At last she had
thought of something really
special she could give the Twins.

She found what she was
looking for, did some
wrapping with
paper and tape,

then dashed back
downstairs with
a square, squidgy
shape...

The party was ruined, or that's how it seemed.

But soon the Twins had the gift of their dreams!

Everyone cheered, then burst into laughter. And the Twins, thanks to Nicky, were...

...nappy ever after!